T·H·E
Three
Little Pigs

RETOLD AND ILLUSTRATED BY

Steven Kellogg

HarperCollinsPublishers

To Peter the Great
with love

Colored inks, watercolors, and acrylics were used for the full-color illustrations.
The text type is 16-point Souvenir Light.

The Three Little Pigs
Copyright © 1997 by Steven Kellogg
Manufactured in China. All rights reserved.
For information address HarperCollins Children's Books,
a division of HarperCollins Publishers,
10 East 53rd Street, New York, NY 10022.

Library of Congress Cataloging-in-Publication Data
Kellogg, Steven.
  The three little pigs / retold and illustrated by Steven Kellogg.
      p.   cm.
  Summary: In this retelling of a well-known tale, Serafina Sow starts her own
waffle-selling business in order to enable her three offspring to prepare for the
future, which includes an encounter with a surly wolf.
  ISBN 0-688-08731-0 (trade) — ISBN 0-688-08732-9 (lib. bdg.)
  ISBN 0-06-443779-5 (pbk.)
  [1. Folklore.   2. Pigs—Folklore.]   I. Title.
PZ8.1.K3Th   1997   96-34434
398.24'529734—dc20   CIP
[E]   AC

Visit us on the World Wide Web!
www.harperchildrens.com
13 SCP 20 19 18 17 16 15 14 13 12

Serafina Sow had three piglets to raise. Their names were Percy, Pete, and Prudence. Money was tight and times were tough until suddenly one night Serafina had an amazing dream. "I want to bring WAFFLES to the world!" she cried.

Serafina bolted an old waffle iron onto a set of wheels and installed a system of tanks, pipes, and hoses.

Then she filled the machine with waffle batter, maple syrup, butter, and powdered sugar.

Each morning at dawn the family pushed Serafina's invention from hamlet to hamlet, delighting passersby with their delicious waffles.

Soon Serafina was able to enroll her piglets at Hog Hollow Academy. As the years passed, they did her proud in the classroom, on the basketball court, and in the school plays.

When graduation day finally rolled around, Serafina turned the waffle business over to her family.

"I shall retire to the Gulf of Pasta," she announced. "If you ever need my help, you can call me there."

The three pigs operated the wafflery while they built new homes nearby. Percy wove straw into a cozy bungalow.

Pete put together a log cabin, and Prudence constructed a brick cottage. The wafflery continued to prosper, and life hummed along happily.

That is, life hummed along happily until a wolf named Tempesto showed up.

"Howdy, Ham. Howdy, Bacon. Howdy, Sausage," he growled. "Butter yourselves and hop on the griddle. I'll eat you for breakfast."

"We only serve waffles," replied Pete nervously. "What flavor would you like?"

"I HATE waffles!" snapped the wolf. "I want YOU!"

Tempesto lunged forward. But in his eagerness to grab the pigs, he overturned the wafflery. Percy, Pete, and Prudence fled to their houses.

A few moments later Tempesto was pounding on the door of Percy's bungalow. "Open up, Pork Chop!" he demanded. "Or I'll huff and I'll puff and I'll flatten this dump!"

Percy frantically scribbled a plea for help on a paper airplane and launched it in the direction of the sheriff's office.

Suddenly, with a blast like a typhoon, Tempesto demolished the straw house, and Percy's possessions were scattered hither and yon across the county.

Percy's paper airplane caught the attention of Sheriff Sheep.

But before he could grab it, Percy's bathtub plunged to earth like a meteorite.

Meanwhile, Percy had reached Pete's cabin one step ahead of the wolf. "Let me in or I'll trash this woodpile!" roared Tempesto.

"No! No! No! Not by the hair of our chinny chin chins!" cried Percy and Pete.

With the force of seventeen chain saws, the wolf reduced
the cabin to sawdust.

The two brothers were blown clear to the brick cottage,
where Prudence whisked them safely inside.

In a few moments the wolf was battering the door.
"Surrender, you cowardly swine!" he bellowed. "Or I'll
huff and I'll puff and I'll blast this pigsty into pebbles!"

"Bombs away!" squealed the pigs. A barrage of watermelons, pumpkins, cantaloupes, grapes, and assorted pastries caught Tempesto completely by surprise and knocked him flat.

The wolf sprang to his feet, foaming with fury.
"This means war!" he hollered. "TOTAL WAR!"

Throughout the rest of the day and all that night,
Tempesto savagely bombarded the little cottage.

But, by the dawn's early light, the frustrated wolf could see that the brick walls were still standing.

"It's time to change tactics," he growled.

Tempesto grabbed a garbage bag and began furiously huffing and puffing.

The bag swelled like a hot-air balloon and soared aloft.
"Set the table, piggies!" cried Tempesto gleefully.
"Breakfast is served!"

Just then a taxicab pulled up to the cottage. The pigs were flabbergasted to see their mother in the backseat.

"I've come to the rescue," announced Serafina.

"How did you know we needed you?" cried the pigs.
Serafina explained that the paper airplane with Percy's
message had fluttered clear to the Gulf of Pasta, where it
landed in her salad.

"Now let's deal with that wolf!" she cried.

Without further delay, the waffle iron was positioned in the fireplace.

Meanwhile, the wolf launched himself down the chimney, screeching, "Here I come, piggies! You'll soon be sausages!"

"No, we won't, wolfie," Serafina cried as the wolf slammed into the red-hot griddle. "*You'll* soon be a WOLFFLE!"

The sizzling wolf staggered from the waffle iron. But before he could catch his breath, the pigs hosed him to the floor with a blast of maple syrup. Then they smothered him in butter, fogged him from head to toe with powdered sugar, and finished him off with a final squirt of syrup.

"I surrender!" he gasped.

Although the emergency was over, Serafina admitted that she was not eager to return to retirement. The news brought cheers from her family. They loaded Tempesto into the taxi and sent him to the Gulf of Pasta in her place.

Soon afterward, Percy, Pete, and Prudence married their
childhood sweethearts.

And it wasn't long before Serafina found herself
surrounded by dozens of grandchildren.

The new family members expanded the business, and soon there were waffleries around the world.

"My dream has come true," sighed Serafina.

As for Tempesto, the waffle iron had steamed the meanness out of him. He gave up crime and spent the rest of his life as a mellow beach bum lolling about on the Gulf of Pasta.